BOOK 2

JUAN GIMENEZ

LEO ROA

AN ODYSSEY BACK IN TIME

Humanoids Publishing™

Translation by Justin Kelly

Graphic design : Thierry Frissen

LEO ROA, BOOK2 : An Odyssey Back in Time

English language edition © 2001 Humanoids Inc. Los Angeles, CA, USA.
Original French edition : 1991 Leo Roa T2 L'Odyssée à Contretemps
© 1995 Les Humanoïdes Associés S.A. Geneva, Switzerland.
All rights reserved.

Humanoids Publishing
PO Box 931658
Hollywood, CA 90093

Printed in Belgium. Bound in France.

ISBN : 0-930652-46-0

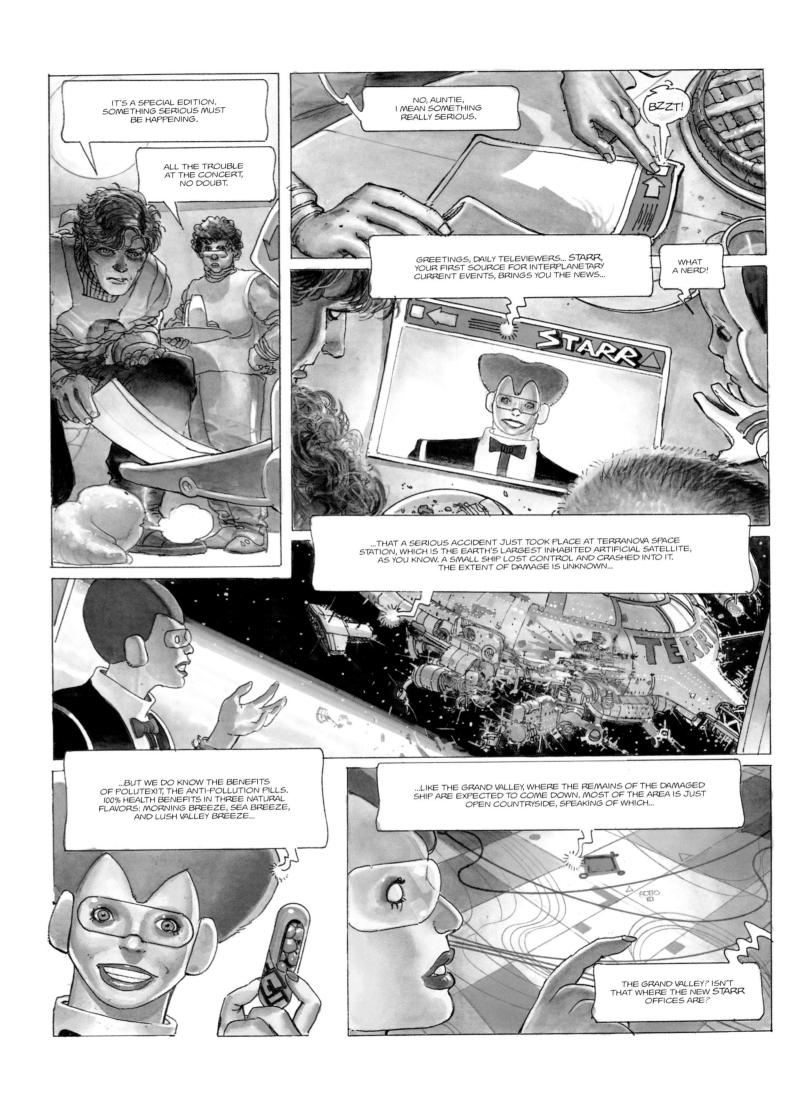

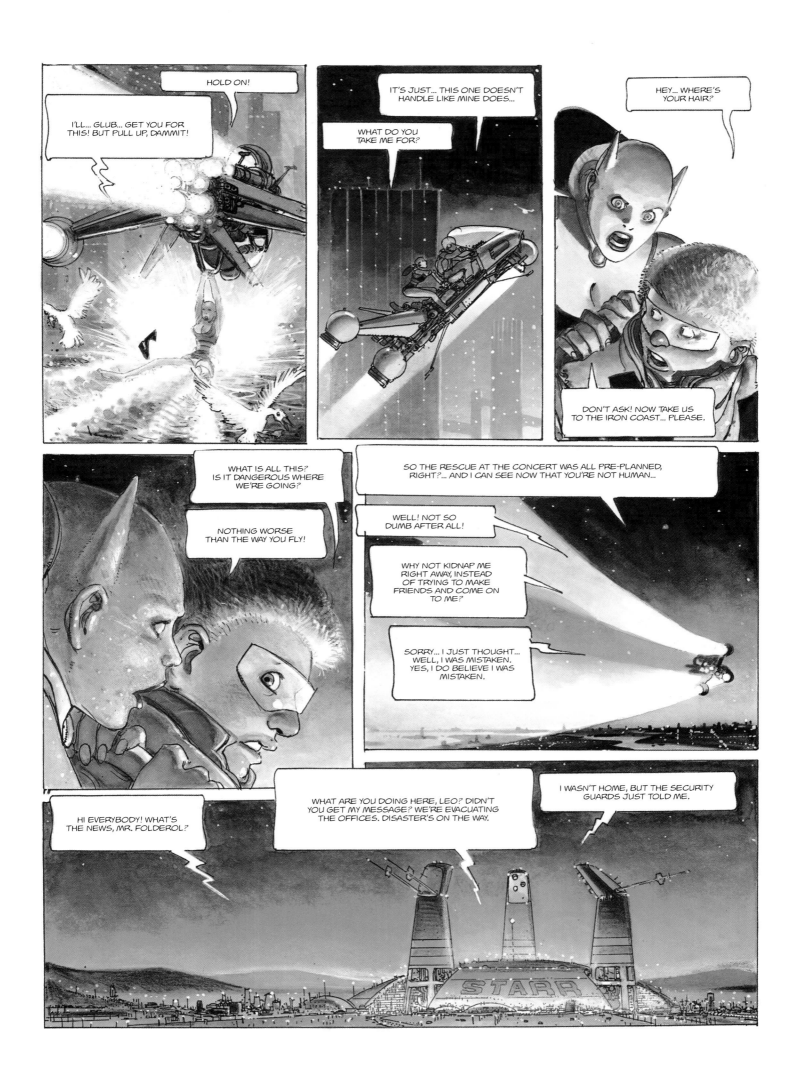

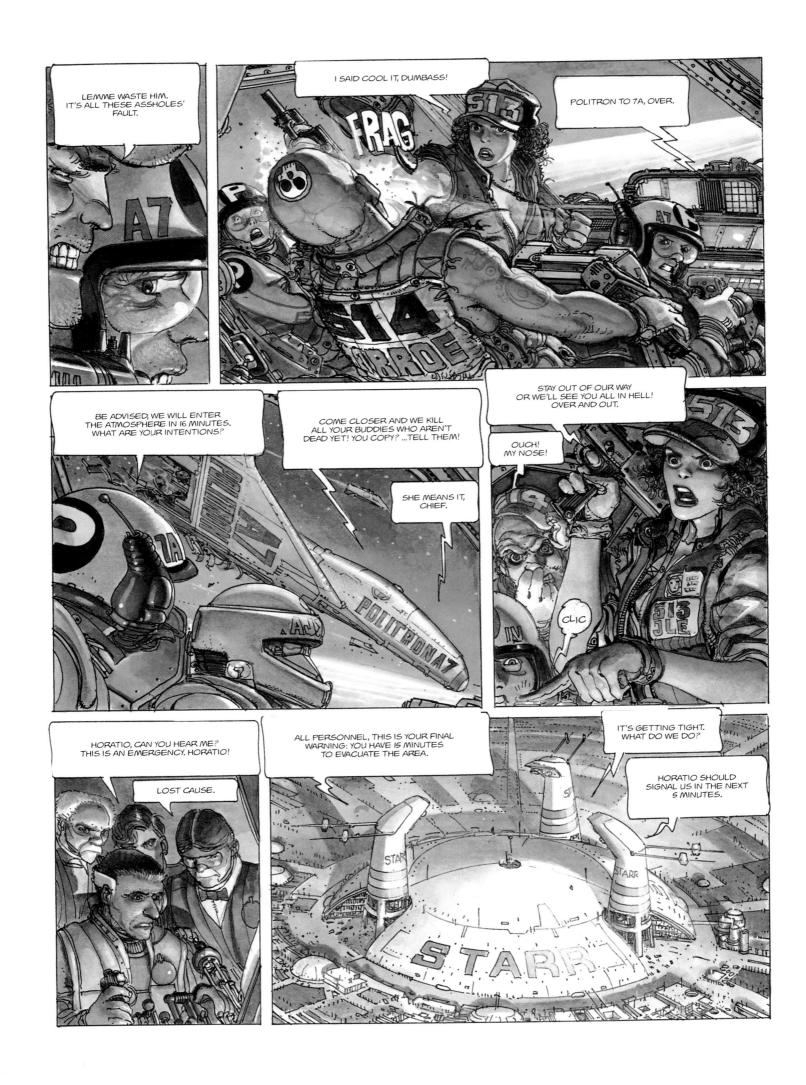

YOU GUYS GO AHEAD. I'LL STAY AT THE COUNTER-T'S CONTROLS. HORATIO WON'T BE LONG.

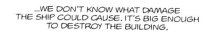

...WE DON'T KNOW WHAT DAMAGE THE SHIP COULD CAUSE. IT'S BIG ENOUGH TO DESTROY THE BUILDING.

...THERE'S NO NEED TO PUT MORE LIVES AT RISK...

IT'S HIM!

HORATIO HERE, DO YOU READ?

...LISTEN, HORATIO, GET READY RIGHT NOW. WE'VE GOT A SITUATION HERE.

WHAT IS IT? WHAT HAPPENED?

NO TIME TO EXPLAIN, BUT WE ONLY HAVE 14 MINUTES TO COMPLETE THE TRANSFER.

LET'S GO!

AND WHAT MAKES YOU SO SURE I'M THE ONE TO HELP YOU?

WATCH THIS TRIDEO CLIP.

SO? WHO IS IT?

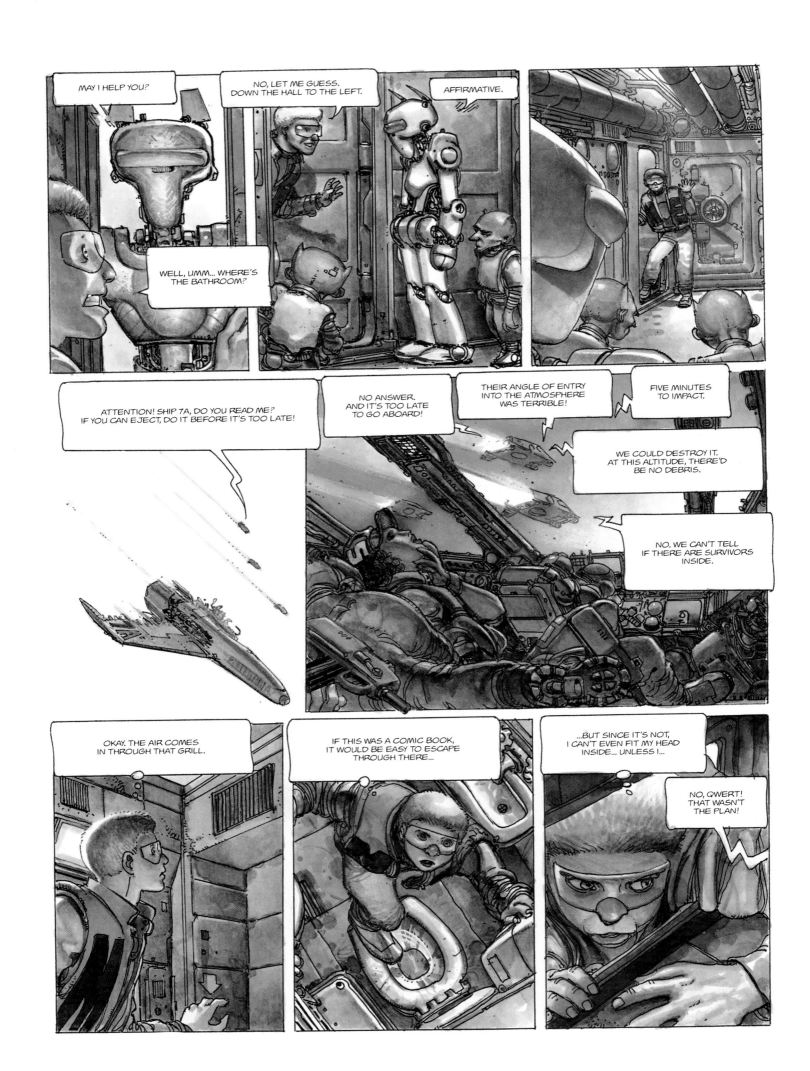

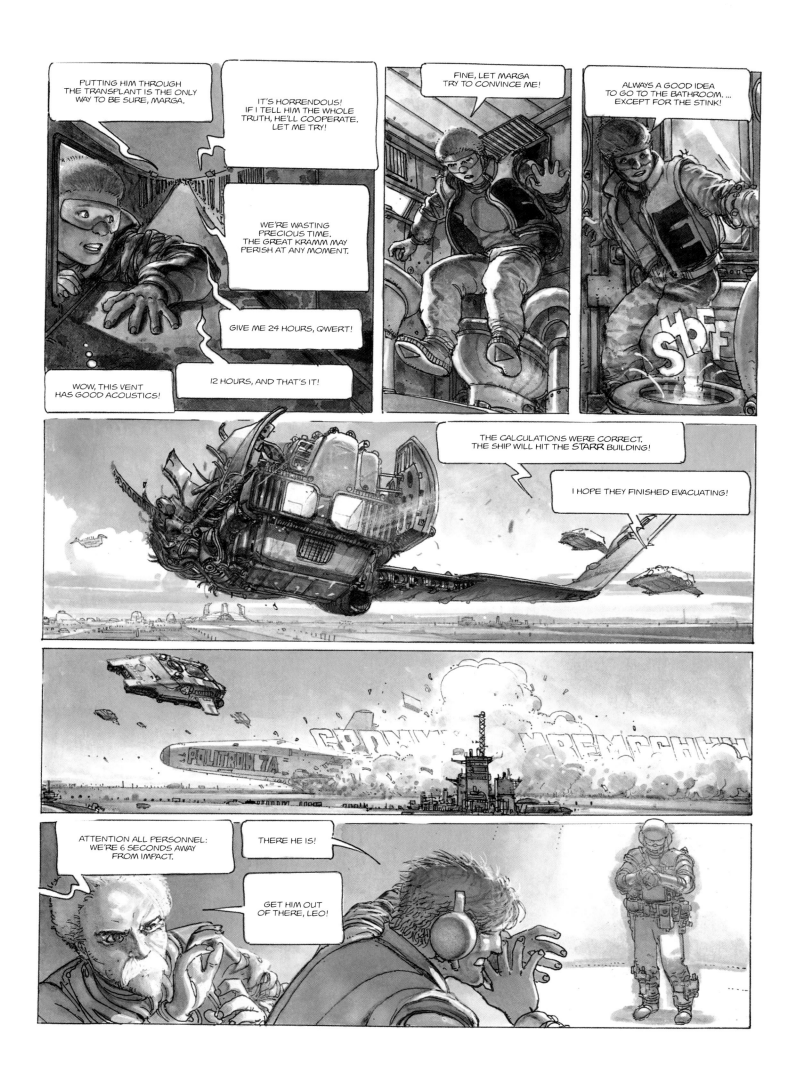

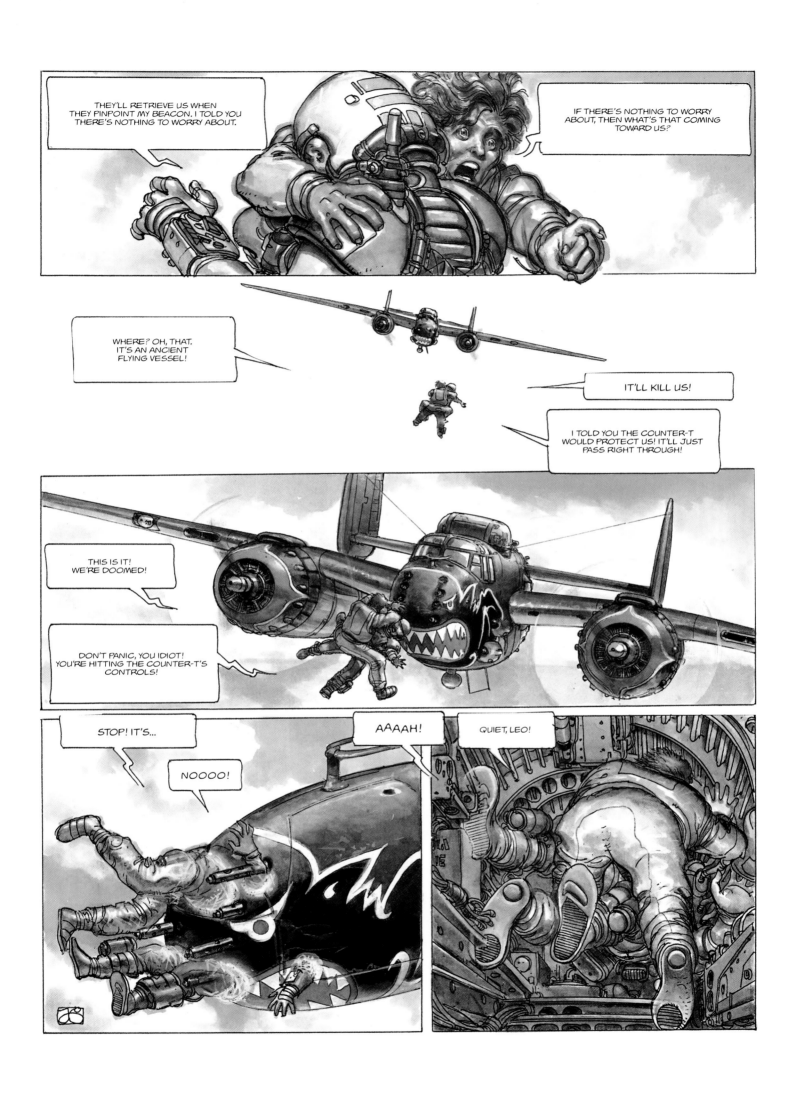

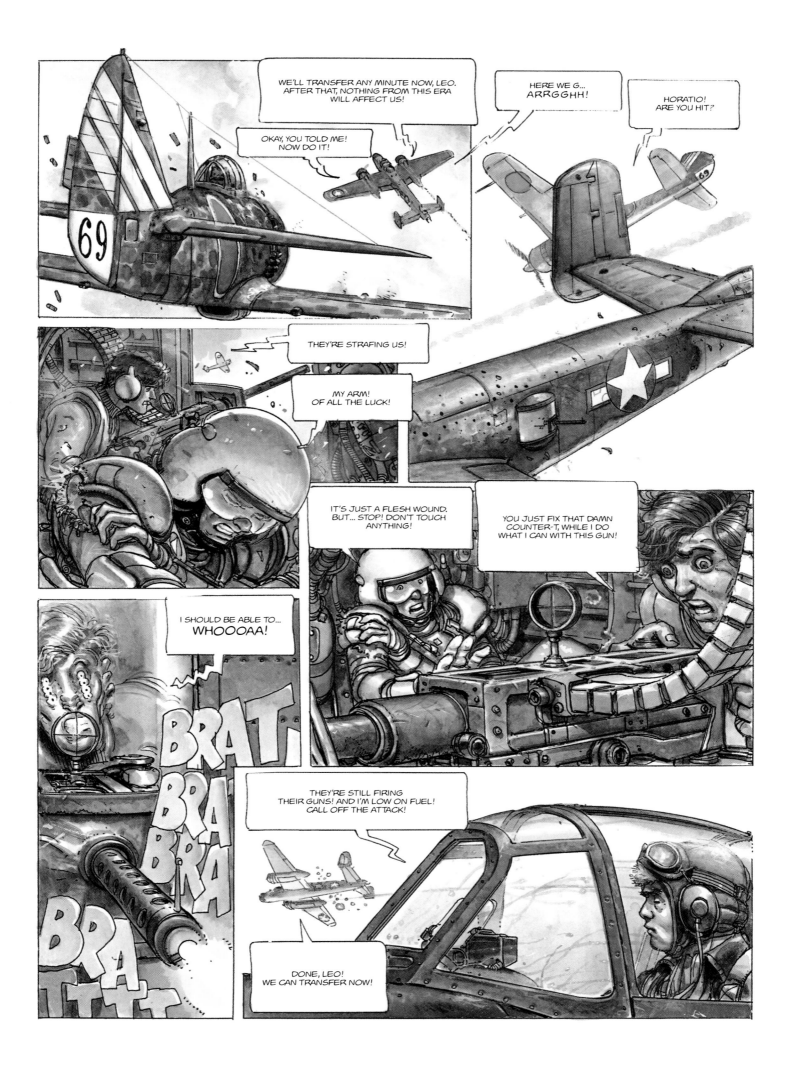

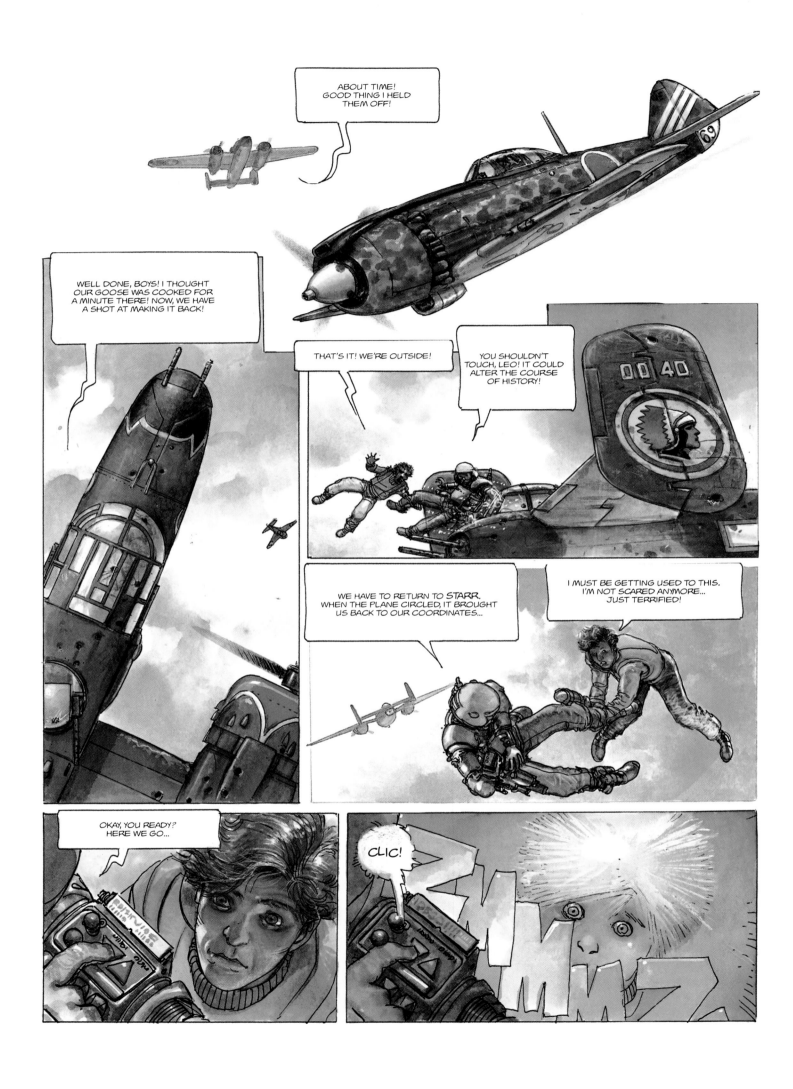

OHH! I'M GETTING TIME-TRAVEL SICKNESS!

LAND! LAND AHOY!

LAND?

IT DIDN'T WORK! WE WENT BACK EVEN FARTHER IN TIME!

TRY IT AGAIN!

DO YOU TRUST HIM TO COOPERATE FULLY? WHAT GUARANTEES CAN MR. MEKENEKULTRANIL GIVE US? HE'S A COMMON EARTHLING. AND STUPID, TOO!

YOU PROMISED TO DO IT WITHOUT THE CEREBRAL TRANSPLANT, QWERT. BESIDES, DON'T FORGET I GIVE THE ORDERS!

I THOUGHT SO! I WON'T LET YOUR CARELESSNESS PUT CENTURIES OF KROTTOM GREATNESS AT RISK. I EXPEL YOU FROM OUR SACRED CAUSE! LOCK HER UP!

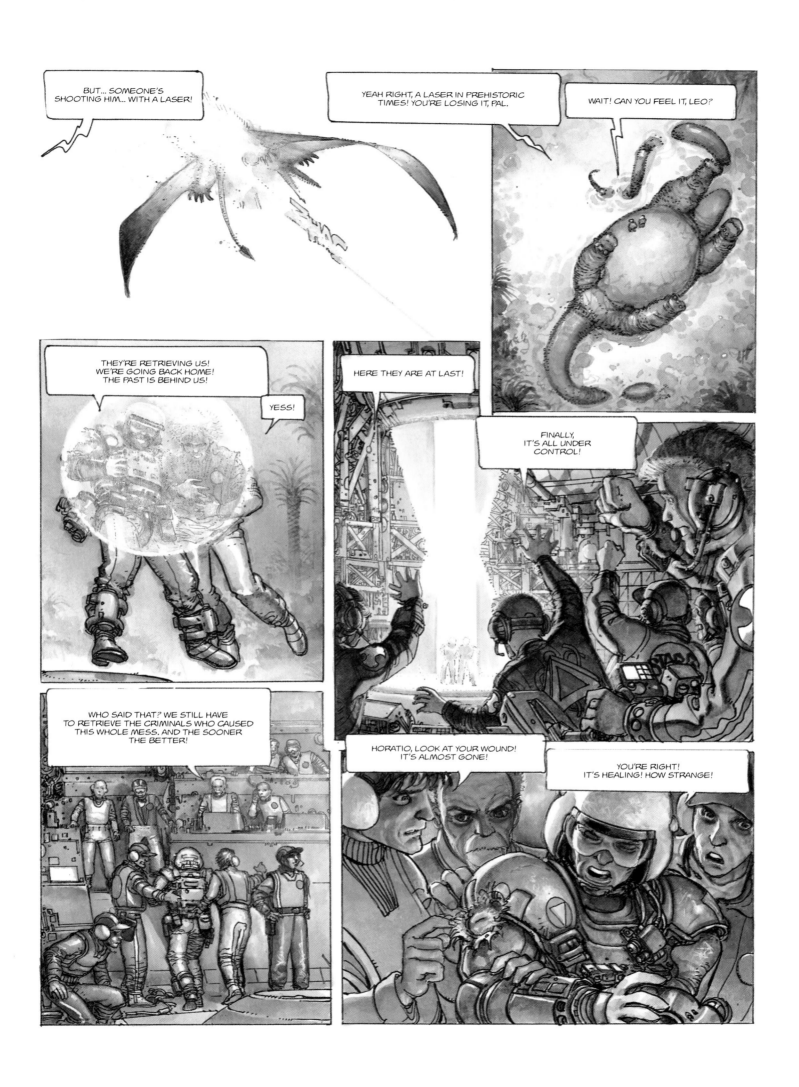

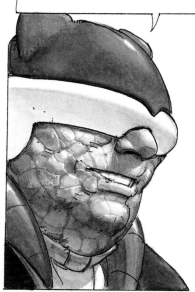
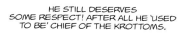

YOUR PRIME MINISTER ESCAPED. I COULDN'T KEEP HER HERE. TOO BAD! YET ANOTHER ERROR ON YOUR PART, ENTRUSTING HER WITH ALL YOUR RESPONSIBILITIES!

YOU... ARE... TOO AMBITIOUS... YOU WILL... LEAD US INTO... CHAOS!

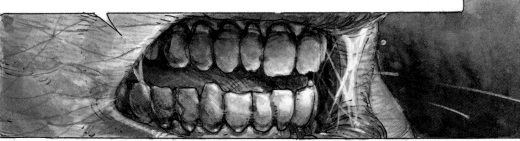

ENOUGH! I'VE BEEN HEARING THAT STUPID TALK FOR YEARS! IT'S TIME TO PUT THINGS BACK THE WAY THEY WERE, AND IT'S TIME I GOT MY HANDS ON THE SCEPTER OF POWER OUR FATHER GAVE YOU INSTEAD OF ME, THE ELDEST SON! JUST BECAUSE HE THOUGHT YOU MORE COMPETENT, MORE INTELLIGENT! WHAT NONSENSE!

THAT'S WHY I MADE A TINY HOLE IN YOUR PROTECTIVE TUNIC, ON THAT DISGUSTING PLANET... NAMED "VISCOSA", I BELIEVE. INHALING A MINUTE AMOUNT OF THAT ATMOSPHERE WAS ENOUGH...

TRAI...TOR! ... COW...ARD!

...TO INFECT YOU WITH THE DISEASE YOU'VE SUFFERED FROM SINCE! AND NOW, BROTHER, I'M GOING TO TRANSPLANT MY BRAIN INTO THE STRONG AND HEALTHY BODY OF YOUR DUMB EARTHLING LOOKALIKE! FROM NOW ON, THE GREAT KRAMM WILL BE ME!

LET ME OUT! MARGA, WHERE ARE YOU? HELP!

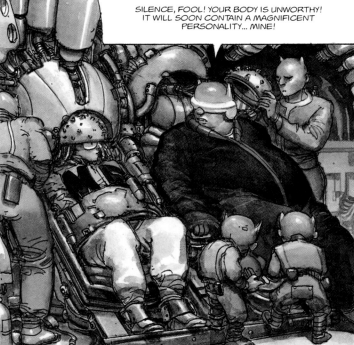

SILENCE, FOOL! YOUR BODY IS UNWORTHY! IT WILL SOON CONTAIN A MAGNIFICENT PERSONALITY... MINE!

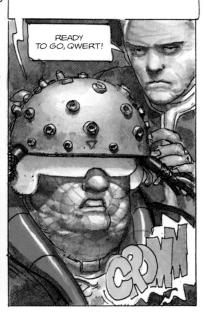

...I SHOULD BE UPSET! I'LL HAVE TO PUT UP WITH YOUR BODY! HOW DEGRADING!

READY TO GO, QWERT!

CRMM

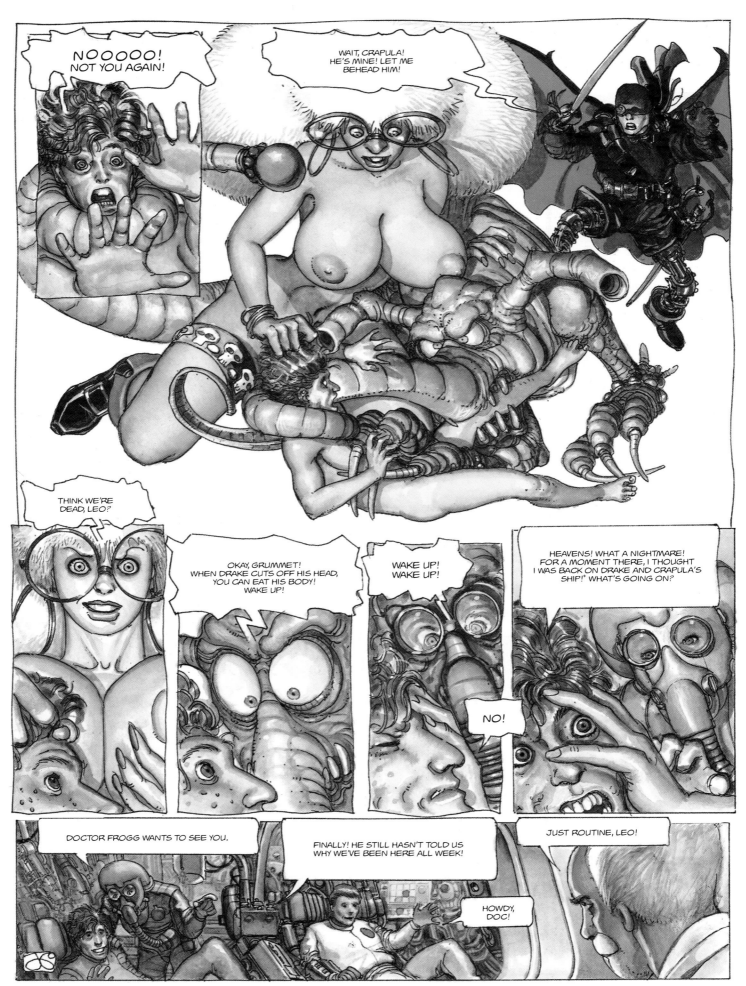

* SEE BOOK I: THE TRUE TALES OF LEO ROA

WATCH OUT! IT HIT...

AS I SUSPECTED!

OW!

HE FELL ON THE ACTIVATION SWITCH!

VWHAP!

THE INSPECTOR! HE'S GOING WITH THEM!

OH!

AAAH!

GROAR!

WAP

YOU OK, INSPECTOR?

WHERE ARE YOU, LEO? I CAN HEAR YOU BUT I CAN'T SEE YOU! THAT HUGE BEAST CAN SEE ME THOUGH!

DON'T WORRY. TOUCH THE COUNTER-T AND IT WILL PROTECT YOU TOO.

ARE YOU SURE? MY GOD!

FOUR DAYS LATER...

MEKE, IF LEO'S FINISHED, WHY'S HE STILL KEEPING US IN AGONIZING SUSPENSE?

DON'T WORRY, MARGA! I KNOW IT'S BIZARRE! BUT LEO SAID HE HAD TO EXPLAIN EVERYTHING TO US HERE AT THE ASTROPORT. FOR SECURIT REASONS!

THERE HE IS, WITH INSPECTOR GONZALEZ!

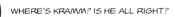

WHERE'S KRAMM? IS HE ALL RIGHT?

BETTER THAN EVER! AS SOON AS YOU'RE READY, YOU CAN JOIN HIM IN THAT SHIP AND FLY BACK TO THE KROTTOMS.

THANKS, LEO! I'LL NEVER BE ABLE TO THANK YOU ENOUGH FOR WHAT YOU'VE DONE FOR US!

IT WAS NOTHING!

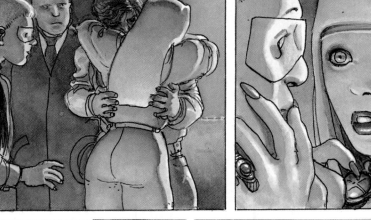

MARGA! I... JUST WANTED TO SAY... I...

PLEASE, MEKE, DON'T TALK!...

GOODBYE, MEKE! THANK YOU! THANK YOU ALL! ...GOODBYE!

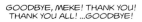

MARGA!

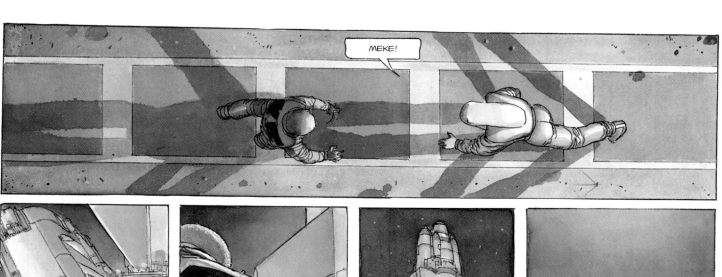

STARR DEVELOPED AN EXTRAORDINARY PROJECT WITH TREMENDOUS JOURNALISTIC POTENTIAL. THE PROJECT, WHICH I HAD TO KEEP SECRET...

...IS TO TRAVEL IN TIME, AND BRING LIVING IMAGES FROM ACROSS HISTORY BACK TO THE PRESENT!

WOW! THAT'S PURE GENIUS!

IT'S GREAT! WHAT A HOOK! SENSATIONAL! BUT... WHAT DOES IT HAVE TO DO WITH THE GREAT KRAMM'S MYSTERIOUS CURE?

ASIDE FROM THE EXTRAORDINARY FEAT OF TRAVELING INTO THE PAST, IT ALSO GAVE US HUMANKIND'S MOST SOUGHT-AFTER DREAM IN HISTORY...

...ETERNAL YOUTH! LIFE WITHOUT LIMITS!

WHAAAT? BUT HOW?

ANY INJURY FROM THE PRESENT SEEMS TO HEAL IN A FEW HOURS WHEN YOU GO BACK INTO THE PAST. I'M STILL NOT SURE HOW, THOUGH.

YOU'RE A BIT SLOW, LEO. IT'S COMMON SENSE! WHEN YOU GO BACK IN TIME, THE CELLS REVERSE THEIR PROCESSES, GET IT?

ME NOT BIG GENIUS LIKE COUSIN MEKE! ALL I KNOW IS...

SORRY, NO OFFENSE. GO ON...

...THAT AFTER THE FUGITIVES HAD BEEN ACCIDENTALLY STRANDED IN TIME FOR TWO WEEKS, WE FOUND THEM TRANSFORMED INTO...

...LITTLE BABIES!

ONCE INSIDE STARR'S LABORATORIES...

THERE'S NO DOUBT ABOUT IT! BLOOD SAMPLES AND GENETIC TESTS PROVE IT'S MACRO AND DEBORAH.

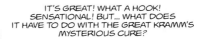

ONE MORE DAY IN THE PAST, AND THEY'D HAVE WINKED OU OF EXISTENCE! UNBORN!

EUREKA! IF YOU TRAVEL REGULARLY INTO THE PAST, YOU DON'T AGE! YOU STAY AT THE SAME BIOLOGICAL AGE AND CAN LIVE AS LONG AS YOU DESIRE!

THAT'S WHEN WE REMEMBERED THE GREAT KRAMM'S PREMATURE AGING. I COULDN'T TELL YOU, BUT WE BROUGHT HIM TO STARR'S LABS.

ALONG WITH A TEAM OF MEDICOBOTS, WE TRANSFERRED HIM TO THE SAME CAVE IN THE SAME ERA WHERE WE FOUND MACRO AND DEBORAH.

...WE APPROXIMATED THAT THREE MESOLITHIC DAYS WOULD BE ENOUGH TO RETURN HIM TO HOW HE WAS BEFORE THE ILLNESS!

LOOK! HE'S REJUVENATING AMAZINGLY FAST!

24 HOURS SHOULD BE ENOUGH!

ONLY HALF-CONSCIOUS, KRAMM DIDN'T NOTICE A THING. WE TOLD HIM HE WAS ON MEDICATION. THEN WE SPILLED THE BEANS ON QWERT. YOU KNOW THE REST.

INCREDIBLE! I CAN UNDERSTAND WHY IT'S SO VITAL TO KEEP IT A SECRET! I WON'T TELL ANYONE, EVEN MY MOTHER, OR MARGA!

...OR MARGA...

WE SHOULD ASSEMBLE THE WHOLE COUNTER-T TEAM AND MAKE SURE THEY KEEP EVERYTHING QUIET! ...AT LEAST FOR NOW!

I'D HATE TO SEE THE RESULTS IF WORD GOT OUT AROUND OUR PLANETARY SYSTEM! WHO DOESN'T WANT ETERNAL YOUTH? OH! INSPECTOR! ON YOUR HEAD...

WHAT'S ON MY HEAD?

AMAZING! THERE'S A HAIR GROWING ON IT! IT WAS BALD BEFORE!

WHAT? IMPOSSIBLE! YOU'RE JOKING, RIGHT?

NO, INSPECTOR! FEEL IT! THERE!

IT IS THERE! IT'S TRUE! I HAVE ONE! A HAIR JUST GREW! IT MUST BE THE EFFECTS OF THE TIME TRAVEL!

...OR EVEN MARGA...

I DON'T KNOW, OUR JOURNEY ONLY LASTED ABOUT 12 MINUTES. BUT I GUESS IT'S POSSIBLE.

A HAIR! I CAN'T BELIEVE IT!

LOOK CAREFULLY! THERE MIGHT BE OTHERS!

LET'S SEE! UHH... NO. IT'S THE ONLY ONE...

TOO BAD...

COME ON, MEKE! ARE YOU STAYING HERE ALL NIGHT? YOUR MOM WOULD WORRY!

WHO KNOWS? MAYBE ONE DAY...

IF WE STAYED A FEW MORE HOURS IN THE MESOLITHIC ERA, I MIGHT HAVE A FULL HEAD OF HAIR BY NOW... WHAT DO YOU THINK, LEO?

BEATS ME, INSPECTOR!

WE'LL MEET AGAIN, MARGA!

COME ON, MEKE! WHAT ARE YOU WAITING FOR?